COLD LAKE ANTHOLOGY
2023

For Bitik
from Dorian
July 2023

Thanks for your
unending support!

♡

♡

Cold Lake Anthology 2023

Burlington Writers Workshop

*Edited by Lauren McGovern,
Janet McKeehan-Medina,
Elaine Pentaleri, Amy Place,
and Nancy Volkers*

Cold Lake Publishing

Contents

From the Editors

Consider the human capacity to endure, to emerge from adversity with resilience and hope. As Nelson Mandela said, "I learned that courage was not the absence of fear but the triumph over it. The brave man is not he who does not feel afraid, but he who conquers that fear." As we face changes, difficulties, and seemingly insurmountable obstacles, we grow stronger and often surprise ourselves with our outcomes.

The stories and poems in *Cold Lake Anthology 2023* reflect upon the human capacity to thrive under challenging circumstances. In his flash fiction piece "The Cracked Parts," Mike Maguilo shares the story of a young boy struggling to come to terms with his own personal challenges. In Dorian Hastings' "Starling Dreams," we find a tale embedded within a tale, each reflecting on loss and grief. Reading the poetry of Nancy Haiduck, we are asked to accept and cherish youth and the loss of it over time. Kerstin Lange's nonfiction story "Phantom Border" captures the reunification of Berlin and reflects profoundly on the outcomes of resilience and hope that history has offered us.

These stories and poems lift us beyond struggle and into a place of renewed possibility.

We hope you enjoy these stories and poems as much as we do. We are so pleased to present the work of the talented writers showcased here in *Cold Lake Anthology 2023*.

The Editors: Lauren McGovern, Janet McKeehan-Medina, Amy Place, Elaine Pentaleri, Nancy Volkers

Mike Magluilo

The Cracked Parts

Mom's frustration with my latest tic escalates to a crack on the head. The abrasive sounds from the back of my throat mimic some baleen distress call and replace the spastic nose scrunches from last week.

She asked me to stop, then handed me the squeeze ball. When that didn't work, she gave me a stick of gum, took her deep breaths and counted to ten. Twice. The fleshy part of her hand snapped me out of it, like when grandpa fixes the fuzzy television with his foot.

I leave the table without being told and let the screen door slam behind me. None of the kids on our block are awake this early, so I sneak up the trunk of Hancock, the conifer Dad estimates is at least as old as grandma.

Within seconds I'm standing on the two-by-fours my cousin Billy laced to one of the lower branches four years ago. These planks of wood were the highest we could climb when we were six years old. They served as our hangout that summer, back when our imaginations were unburdened by the knowledge a tree house required walls and a roof. Billy no longer climbs with me. I don't give him enough space. I'm clingy.

I've been hiding in the higher branches this summer and soon reach the spot Billy calls the Bleacher Seats. I'm eye-level with our roof and can see the second floor of the Wilson's house across the street. Resting will invite my noisy tic to return and blow my cover, so I keep climbing.

The gaps between branches grow bigger up here. I stretch my arms until my shoulders burn, barely able to grip the branches above.

I don't want to stop. Freedom from my body's impulses and all the nagging about things I can't control propels me higher. My feet provide enough lift to wrap my fingers around the next branch. A squirrel looks up from her acorn, tilting her head to watch me scoot my legs up onto the limb with the grace of a bear cub. I study my cracked, bloody hands and understand the squirrel's amusement.

I gaze past Hancock's needles at the big blurry world stretching to the horizon. The familiar streets of my paper route lead my eyes to our church, and the world becomes less threatening when I can touch my school with the tip of my finger.

I inch along the trunk like a caterpillar and kick my legs onto the highest branch with serious effort. The sky surrounds me, and the clouds appear closer. The only thing to hold onto is the trunk, which I hug tightly, spooked by the lack of cover up here.

The top of the tree is a powerful place. Boy, will it be great to tell Billy how far I made it today – he'll never tease that out of me. I make the mistake of looking down and see how much I have to lose. I could silence the grunts from my throat and the noises in my head by simply loosening my grip. The thought causes the branches below to spin, and the concentric force of vertigo tugs at me as I squeeze the trunk more tightly.

Mom calls my name from the screen door. My voice cracks when I respond. Unable to hear my whimper, she steps out the house and gazes up and down the neighbors' backyards.

Letting go would free me from the shame of my disorder, but ending my suffering would destroy my family. All I want is to get back for breakfast and use my arms and gym shoes to control my slide down the trunk.

I pause again at the Bleacher Seats. Pushing myself to a scary place today consumed the attention and anxiety my curse preys upon. I learned I don't need to kill it, I just need to find something new to frighten me tomorrow. Blood oozes down the soft, fleshy sides of my forearms, but the cracks that drove me up this tree have healed because the woman who never ignores an opportunity to fix my flaws noticed I was missing and came looking for me.

N. G. Haiduck

Sestina

Red patent leather high heels click
like castanets on cobblestone.
Across the way a man so young
tenders a rose as red
as guitars galloping ahead.
Now she's not in any hurry.

Today she's not in a hurry.
Elbows on the café table, she clicks
her glass to his. The years ahead
could skip across the sky like stones.
She writes, "Yo también" in lipstick red,
just because she's young.

Just because they're young,
they're not in any hurry.
Dreaming riddles, drinking red
Sangria, body and souls click.

In her hair the rose, in his hand a stone,
the summer sun burns overhead.

Presenting the ring with a bow of the head,
just because she's beautiful and young,
he offers more than a birthstone.
Can this moment be stopped? Hurry.
Wait: The photographer clicks.
The horizon turns hummingbird red.

The city dust in the light spins red.
Laughter, a song, touching heads,
an embrace, a kiss, a click
for the check. Once you are young.
Free from uncertainty, they hurry.
Other lives lead to ash and stone.

On her finger a ruby stone,
the slanting sun still red.
They want to get home in a hurry.
The apartment is just ahead.
Two lovers happy and young
like the rhythm her high heels click.

A street light clicks. The cobblestones
usher the young past cafés umbrella red
to shorter days ahead. Hurry.

N.G. Haiduck

Uncovered

Traipsing high on a mountain ridge
with girlfriends on a hot summer day,
how easily I shed my faded jeans, my tie-dyed shirt,
and swinging loose from my brassiere, kicked
cotton panties off my hiking boots.
My giggling pals, my court, carried my discarded clothing
like regal robes and I laughed like the Queen of May.

Ah, freedom! Ambling naked in the sun,
a lovely mirage I must have been
to the two guys suddenly sauntering toward us.
My court expected me to hide behind a tree,
but I was young and breathing mountain air.
I met the strangers' pretty eyes and nodded cheerily,
maintaining my position in the nude until they passed.

Now barefoot on the worn carpet,
breasts dangling over dresser drawers,

clutching my pajamas with the leopard print,
I catch my husband's gaze reflected in the mirror,
his book and glasses set beside the bed, and almost trip
pulling up the draw-string bottoms,
not wanting him to see a dimple or gray hair
he may not have seen before. I fumble
with the tiny buttons, shivering, though the room is warm.
He laughs, throws back the quilt, reaches to dim the light,
opens his arms, "I know you. Come here."

Mark
Pendergrast

Lion

The ant lion,
fierce mandibles
at bay in his sandpile,
awaits the wayward ant,
scrapes furious particles
for the landslide meal.

On the boy's hand,
it tickles out
a summer tune.

Starling Dreams

Jake came over to console me a month after my dog died. I woke up in the early hours, couldn't sleep, turned the radio to a public station talk show. The host was interviewing a country music singer about his latest album, tour. I came in in the middle of the interview, I was groggy, it was background noise. Then he sang a song about his good old dog who died in his arms, and great heaving sobs exploded from deep within me. And it didn't stop, only the heaving, breaking waves of sobs, with no tears. I couldn't beat it back, I could hardly speak on the phone, only, "My dog, my sweet old dog."

So he rushed over. What a kind person. He had to let himself in. He had keys because he would take care of mail, newspaper, the dog when I was out of town. Finally I calmed down enough, so we went to the living room and sat on the sofa. He made us some sweet warm milk and toast.

"I don't know where that came from, Jake! I didn't cry when he died!"

"It's life, Susan," he said, "it's crazy times."

"I have to confess, I never cried like that for any person..." I said.

"You don't ever know what love is till you have a dog," he said.

"Well, that's true. That love lasted longer than any relationship I ever had—fifteen years! Sickness and health. Hurricanes and fires. What hurts the most is what I didn't do for him. He was so sweet and nurturing, he wanted a doggie pal, which I could never supply. I kept meaning to get him some doggie stairs so he could get up on the bed with me when he got old, which is where he really wanted to be. I could've done that at least for that sweet pure soul," and I felt tears welling up. "I can still feel his rough fur in my fingers, and in the dark I can feel his presence, almost hear him snuffling..."

"I'll tell you a story," he said. That's why I called Jake; he always has a story.

"You remember me telling you about my ever-so-great aunt, Franziska, born in Vienna in 1821, her diary and testimonies that have passed down through the family. Well, there is one story, a fairy tale almost, though generations have sworn to the absolute truth of it. At least, that is the truth as she wrote it—I've read it with my own eyes. The ink on the pages now faded to brown. She wrote it in her old age, encouraged to write it down by her favorite niece, my ever-so-great grandmother, Theresia. This is Franziska's story—or Franzi, as they called her when she was a child." Out of his messenger bag, he pulled a Victorian sort of box, covered with red satin and black lace, and out of the box came a binder. "The original manuscript of her memoirs is in the bank vault," he explained. "What I have here is the translation." And he paged through till he found the place the story began.

One day, as I was playing in the garden of our house in the Vienna suburbs, I found a baby starling on the ground, screaming and squawking. It had barely fledged and had fine pin feathers. I ran to find Papa, but he could find no nest, nowhere to return it to, and rather than leave it to its fate, we brought it inside. I was so excited! A baby of my very own! So much more interesting than my other baby dolls, though I often felt pangs of guilt at neglecting them. I would pile them in bed with me at night and sing them to sleep to make up for it.

I called my bird "Kiki" because that was the sound she made when we found her – she cried her own name to lead us to her.

Papa knew everything. He said we must feed it and warm it, so we kept it in the kitchen inglenook, in a special nest made of wool shreds. Cook complained quite a bit, I can tell you. I was underfoot all the time because Kiki needed to be fed every thirty minutes, and sometimes Cook even had to fill in because, well, she was there and I couldn't be there *all* the time! I did have to eat, and since it was the most beautiful time of May, Papa and I had our walks most every day in the woods just beyond the garden gate, and I had to have my afternoon lie-down, Mama insisted on that. At least they don't have to be fed throughout the night, Mama said that was a blessing. She knew only too well because Ludi was not yet sleeping through the night himself. She was tired a lot in those days. She said Kiki could teach me a lot about being a mother.

I thought I loved Ludi when he was born. His fuzzy little baby-smelling head! But in truth, Kiki was much more interesting. All Ludi did was eat and sleep, I had to "Be quiet, Franzi, for goodness sake!" With Kiki, I was her all, and she was all mine.

Papa showed me how to make Kiki's food, with a bit of rabbit, porridge, a boiled egg, and boiled apple all ground together and warmed to just the right temperature. Sometimes we added cooked carrots or parsnips. I used my tiny doll spoons to feed her. I felt so proud to see her grow and grow. She had an adorable pompadour of fine feathers on top of her head. It was so sweet, I wanted to make her a tiny bonnet with some ribbons to match mine, but Papa said that would be a bad idea as she was so small a bonnet might crush her.

Some days Papa had to go into town to attend to business. On those days, Mama would leave Ludi with Nurse and come to the kitchen with me to help feed Kiki.

Those were very happy days. After a few weeks, we could put down seeds and chopped nuts and bits of fruit for her to peck. We made a bath for her in a shallow dish and put it in the garden in the sun so she could learn to drink and to keep herself clean. We had to watch out carefully for those bad cats, though, who would make a mouthful of her. By then, her feathers were almost fully grown out.

Also, Mama and Papa were happier. They were so sad when Maestro Beethoven died, they even named our new baby Ludwig, though he should have been named Maximilian, after Papa's father. Papa even took me to watch the funeral procession, but from Uncle Willi's balcony, though he went to the church himself. It was such a beautiful sunny day, but everybody was very sad. There were so many people in the funeral procession, I lay down on the floor and went to sleep. But by June, Mama even wanted to play her violin again and we had concerts sometimes, the warm summer air blowing through the house, and Papa would dance with me, swinging me in a waltz.

Kiki grew stronger and even began to sing with us! She would ride around on my shoulder (though Nurse made me wear a special shawl because of her pooping). She began to fly around, and I was afraid to take her outside because I didn't want her to fly away. But there was nothing to worry about on that score – I soon discovered that she didn't want to leave. She might fly up into a tree, but she would come right back to my shoulder. I began to take her on walks with Papa.

One day I remember, Papa and I were on the path we took most often that took us past a small cottage across a field. I especially remember the profusion of plants and flowers and we would sometimes see the old woman who lived there tending her garden. That day, as we were passing, we heard a ruckus and a lot of shouting, something like "Witch, witch, we'll toss you in a ditch!" and the old woman screeching back. Papa got quite consternated and hid me in some bushes. "You remember how we talked about the baby rabbits and how their parents taught them to be very still and quiet? Well, you must do that for me now. Be very still and quiet here, and I will be back directly." And he went off. Sure enough, he came back quickly enough and said that some boys had been tormenting old Amelie but that he had run them off with a thrashing and told them they would hear from him very soon!

By the end of summer, Mama and Ludi would even come with us. Usually we would go to our family chalet in the Alps with Uncle Willi and his tribe for the month of August, but Mama was still not strong enough for the trip south and Papa didn't want to leave her. Papa made a special sling to carry Ludi and he would hold Mama's hand on the paths so she wouldn't fall. We would sing – Papa had a wonderful yodeling voice, and to hear Kiki mimic him! We would laugh so hard, we could hardly speak!

By then, Ludi was becoming more interesting. I could make him laugh by making silly noises and sometimes Nurse would let me feed him his gruel. The way he would open his little mouth as I brought the spoon close reminded me of Kiki's early days.

Soon it was fall, and then the autumn rains. Finally, one day was very fine – sunny but still a bit blustery, so Kiki and I went out into the garden. Oh how I wish I never had! Kiki was flitting around the trees and I was making a small village in the dirt when suddenly a strong gust of wind blew through. I heard a small squawk and sickening thud, and looked up to see Kiki plummeting downward.

The wind had blown her against the stones of the house. I ran over to find her, and there she was, lying in the grass. I had tied little red strings around her feet, like laces, to decorate them and I could see them only too well, matching the thin stream of blood running from her beak.

I gathered her up into my apron and ran to find Papa, screaming, "Papa, Papa, Kiki is hurt, you must fix her!"

But Papa said she was dead, it had happened so quickly that it hadn't hurt her (I found *that* small consolation!) He arranged a glorious funeral, he said it would be to the bird world what the funeral of Maestro Beethoven was to the music world. It wasn't nearly so grand, and I didn't care anyway, I only cared that my beloved Kiki was gone.

Things only went from bad to worse that winter. Mama and then Ludi sickened, and they died too, leaving Papa and me in the winter darkness, all alone. The funeral was horrid. Far worse than the one for Kiki. Something wicked came over me at the cemetery and I threw quite the tantrum, threw myself into the dirt, kicking and screaming like a demon. I heard Uncle Willi admonish Papa later, that he should never have taken me to the actual burial – two graves, one very tiny – and for once Papa had to admit that Uncle Willi was probably right.

There was no music, no happiness anywhere to be found.

We went to stay with Uncle Willi for Christmas, but Papa spent most days in his room. At least it was warm and cheerful, with Uncle Willi and Auntie Liesl and their herd of noisy children. I sometimes forgot how sad I was. After New Year's we returned home. Papa said Uncle Willi didn't believe in educating girls so we would stay at home. (I guessed much later that he had thought of perhaps leaving me with the family so I wouldn't be so lonely.) Mama had already taught me how to read and write and play the piano, but he found a governess for me, an elderly widow (well, she seemed quite elderly to me, but I realize now she was probably in her fifties and quite vigorous!), Madame Leclaire, who could teach me French and mathematics and geography and all kinds of other things. Then, by the end of February it was my birthday, but it was all quite sad. We went to visit with Uncle Willi and the family and Papa took me out to buy special pastries, but we returned home much as we had left it. He got me a little dog, but it howled all the time and I wanted nothing to do with it. It just didn't bring me joy the way Kiki had.

The winter dragged on and on. I would often cry and carry on. One day, as Papa put me to bed, I told him, "I can't remember Mama and Ludi! I can't remember her voice!" and cried hysterically. He was so upset. He got Mama's violin and sat there in the dark, playing lullabies for me.

I know I caused Nurse and Madame Leclaire no end of grief. I overheard Madame say to Nurse one day, "Poor little mite," and that's how I began to think of myself – "I'm a poor little mite," I would tell myself. Madame would comfort me and say me that hard work was an antidote to sadness, and explained to me the history and meaning of the word "antidote." Papa stayed in town quite a lot. Cook would take me into the kitchen often and teach me how to make cookies and our daily bread, and even to dress the game that Old Peter would bring us. Finally it was spring, and then warm enough for Papa and me to take our walks again. In August, we went to the chalet in Semmering with Uncle Willi and his brood. The long sunny days, with the healthy peasant food we enjoyed there, the fresh fruits and cream, were restorative, as they should be.

On the way home, we stopped in the capital with Uncle Willi for a few days, especially to visit the new animal that was all the rage that summer at the Royal Menagerie of the Schönbrunn palace – a giraffe! The Viceroy of Egypt had sent it as a special gift to our emperor. Uncle Willi said it was a cross between a camel and a leopard, which Papa said wasn't possible. But when I saw it, I had to believe Uncle Willi for once, it was so odd to look at! We even bought a Giraffentorten, which all the bakers were selling to commemorate the event.

Then it was back home, anticipating a lonely fall and winter.

One afternoon, in my forced post-prandial lie-down, I woke from a dream of Kiki. It was so real! She was back on my shoulder, her fine black and speckled feathers glinting in the sunshine, singing with me, pecking around in the dirt while I built my little village in the garden. And then I awoke. Papa was away. I ran out of the house and into the garden and even that wasn't enough consolation, I ran out of the garden and into the woods. I ran without much knowing where I was going, overcome by grief, and finally, exhausted, sat on a log by the way. I didn't realize it at the time, but it was near the cottage of old Amelie. She saw me, shivering, swiping at the tears with muddy little hands.

"What would your Papa say if he knew you were out here, crying and carrying on!"

"Papa has gone to Prague for business and won't be home till next week!" I sobbed.

She put her arm around me and led me into her hut. It was tiny and warm, with bread just out of the oven. She brought me into the shed and showed me how to milk her goat, Mimi, then we took the warm milk and she made me cocoa with it, along with a slab of fresh bread, buttered and toasted.

"Now, tell me all about your sorrows," she said.

I told her about Kiki and my dream. "I wish I could have Kiki with me, just for one day," I sighed.

"Your wish is granted. Look out your window tomorrow at dawn," said old Amelie. She hitched Mimi up to the goat cart, wrapped me in a warm blanket, and trundled me home, leaving me in the arms of Nurse, who tutted and fussed.

The next morning, at dawn, as instructed, I ran to the window in my room. There was Kiki, pecking at the glass and waiting patiently for me to let her in. I knew it was her because she was still wearing her little red laces!

Such a happy reunion! She talked and sang and flitted about! We rushed into the garden, and it was such a beautiful day, it was like summer again, balmy but still with the wine scent of autumn leaves. We set off in a different direction this time, walking past the pond and across the meadow, then along the brook. There was a rustic bench, so we sat down to rest. I wanted to make the most of my day with Kiki, the day Amelie had promised me!

We were sitting there singing, Kiki perched on my finger, when down the path came a man. He didn't look well. His complexion was gray, tiny round glasses perched on a round nose. He had a walking stick, and his overcoat swung heavy around him, in spite of the warm day.

"What's this? Have you taught your bird to sing?" He stopped short and looked at us. "Do you mind if I sit a bit to listen?"

I wasn't afraid. We never saw strangers, so I had never gotten warnings about talking to them. This wasn't the city. He seemed so interested in our music, so we sang a bit more, Kiki like a flute accompanying me. Soon he joined in, and soon I was telling him my story – about how Kiki died and I missed her so much, and about old Amelie and her promise.

"I have Kiki again for the day, and I am going to make the most of it!"

He laughed, and looked a bit cheerful for the first time. "You have a lovely voice," he said. "Are you going to be a singer? I wrote a song about a pigeon once, would you like to hear it?"

"Don't you have a song about a starling?" I asked. "We would much rather hear that!"

"Ho, ho! You are right! Pigeons don't really carry a tune, do they? Well, I will have to write one for you!" and he began to whistle, a sweet, lovely plaintive melody.

"But what are the words?" I asked.

"I will have to ask one of my poet friends for the words. I will play the melody for him, and he will give me the words," he answered.

He sat a bit longer and then heaved himself up. "Thank you, my dear, for sharing your joy. You really do have a lovely voice. I predict one day you will be famous," he said, and was off.

We wandered along the brook for a bit longer and then I had to go and share Kiki with old Amelie! We sang for her too, and then the shadows grew longer. It was still fall, of course, and though the day was warm, it was short. Amelie had a cup of milk for me and some crumbs for Kiki. On the way home, Kiki flew up and disappeared among the trees and I never did see her again. It was such a sweet day, one I will never forget.

Papa came home, and said he had something to tell me, someone he wanted me to meet.

I soon met her, a lovely lady, and soon she and Papa were married, and soon there were other children. I did become a famous singer, traveling the world.

Many decades later, after that day with Kiki, my agent came to me with a song he said I should put in my repertoire. It was called "The Shepherd on the Rock." I looked over the score – something about it seemed so familiar!

"Play it for me, Walter," I directed my accompanist.

It wasn't till that evening that I realized, it was the same tune the man by the brook had whistled for me! The day Kiki came home. The musician who himself would be dead, too young, in a few months. The song wasn't about Kiki after all, his poet friends had written instead about a shepherd longing for his love far away. But it captured all the joy and longing of Kiki and my love for her, the loss of my mother – all that it expressed.

Franz Schubert said, "When I wished to sing of love, it turned to sorrow. And when I wished to sing of sorrow, it was transformed for me into love." When I learned that quote, it pierced me to my heart. The core of love is sorrow; the core of sorrow is love. I still dream of Mama and Ludi, and of Kiki. And of Papa too, who is now long dead. Will I ever put sorrow aside? Probably not, because to put sorrow aside, I would have to put love aside, too.

"Here ends this part of the story," Jake said.

"What is that?" I asked, "'The Shepherd on the Rock'?"

"One of Schubert's many lieder. He wrote it shortly before he died – in November 1828 – for a young soprano. It's about...well, I guess there's a shepherd standing on a rock overlooking a valley, thinking about lost love, and he's singing into the ravines. 'Deep grief consumes me, I'm so lonely,' he sings. 'The song sounded so longingly through the forest, It sounded so longingly through the night, That hearts are drawn to heaven, With wonderful power.'"

And then he sang some of it for me, in German. It captured all the pain and joy of love for me, at that moment at least.

"Jake, you are a true musician. Thank you."

"Anytime, my dear. Now, I'd better get home. Robert will be wondering where I am."

He left me quiet, pondering on this strange and mystical tale of a young girl, still heartsore for my old dog, but able at last to sleep.

Sharon Lopez
Mooney

Eavesdropping on the Redwoods

I heard a gaggle of tough young redwoods
trying to get the ancients' attention
but the elder trees were not interested in prattle,
the youngins played in the quick-step breeze
limbs raised cowboy-on-a-bronc style
flexing boughs wildly, whipping in the wind.

The whippersnappers did not give up,
swinging branches
conducting rhythm for afternoon westerlies,
taunting the delicate saplings
to be pushy, to tickle the big guys
with itchy sprouts through every crack, crevice.

I hesitated standing on the soft cushion

of their wooded home,
the Redwoods didn't bother with me
didn't care if I understand their symphony,
swaying though their green fingers
in keys and timbre foreign to my ears,

They seemed quite happy to not notice me at all.

Sharon Lopez
Mooney

Brush Strokes on Eighty

Paint stroke #1

a shock of *alone*
arrives in late evening
when there's chill on the house
and silence lingers with cobwebs,
it doesn't startle, doesn't break open,
it stands still, face to me, stark
but alive and assured

seven beats of frozen silence
facing my self's new countenance
reflected back in *alone's* solid stance
i let go daily, but cannot revive lost loves,
cannot embody my disappeared agility,

standing side by jowl with another
does not assuage this solitary singleness

i am *alone*
my attentive children surround me
with pleasures of inclusion
but i live a secret
they cannot share
i am *alone*
and we have settled in together

Paint stroke #2

She turned back from the curb
a house
her house
forty years ago a middle age woman
wedded again with a new marriage bed
a new garden, new habits to build

twenty years ago, he took
his final leave, stolen from her
from the inside out,
snatching breath, fraying their life,
the slowness of the rip
still burns along the edges

ten years ago, she can see it still,
collective concern for her public fall,
she pushed against their good intentions
cutting into her days, ragged remains of her time

accidental lacerations to ego still tender,
she leans against the car defeated

the precious nest that enfolded her life
worn bare to the borders of the porch
the screen door aslant on loose hinges
dingy drapes still hanging dutifully
furniture dissolving like hunks of bread
as she opens the car door she can't look back

Remember, 'retirement' home,
not hospice! She repeats over and over
as her daughter slips through traffic
up over the only big hill in town
and down onto the oneway drive
delivering her to the end of her ride

Paint stroke #3

we watched my genial mother-in-law
mutate every hour she stayed alive
into ripe resentment of what
the years had brought her to,
she sat silent and angry
in the midst of the children
she had made a life of,
she refused to embrace
alone, who
she knew
had stolen

so much away
from her

but now with my own visit
from *alone,*
i opened the door
instinctively
let her in
nakedly unprepared
she has come
not as guest
but as new inmate,
she brings
nothing with her
she leaves no footprint
she is *alone.*

Brian Gardam

Arland Reel

For a few years in my twenties, I worked at the state psychiatric center. When I tell people this, they often give me the benefit of assuming I had a therapeutic role, providing counseling and comfort to the residents. In fact, I hardly ever saw a patient, unless they were competent enough to sign some form I needed. I was a Resource and Reimbursement Agent. It was my job to find out what financial resources patients had and then take most of it away from them to reimburse the state for the cost of their care.

It was a job consumed with paperwork. Obtaining birth certificates, completing applications for Social Security, disability, Medicaid and Medicare, and veterans' benefits – these are what filled my day. There were some challenges in doing this, but before I was there a year the work became deadly routine. Those were the days before psychoactive medications made it possible, or provided an excuse, to discharge people with mental disabilities from the big inpatient facilities. The psychiatric center then housed more than a thousand patients. For me and the other R&R Agents, most of them were only names and numbers. It was necessary labor, I suppose, but terrifically boring.

I tell you this not to justify my actions, but to give you some context to explain my motives.

For diversion, I got into exploring the small towns in the area on the weekends. I enjoyed learning about their history and the lives of the people who lived there. One Saturday, I was wandering around the cemetery of a riverside village, looking at the names and dates of the men and women who had once been the life of the community. For some reason I stopped at a small marker laid into the grass.

The marker read "ARLAND REEL, 1/5/18-3/6/18, BELOVED SON OF CLAUDE AND MARIE REEL."

It was a sad little stone. Little Arland had only made it to two months of age. Quite likely, he was one of the thousands killed by the 1918 Spanish Flu epidemic. I felt sympathy for the grieving of the infant's parents. But then an idea struck me. I had found birth certificates for people with less information than was contained in the engraving. The second thought was that, since Arland had died before the advent of Social Security, there would never have been a Social Security number issued in his name. What if I could give little Arland a life – at least on paper?

I didn't want to be totally callous about it. When visiting the county clerk's office for work, I spent some time looking up records of Claude and Marie Reel. I satisfied myself that they were both deceased, and sadly had left no living offspring.

The next steps were routine. After obtaining Arland's birth certificate, I applied for a Social Security number on his behalf. Inspired by his last name, I filled out that he had spent his working life as a self-employed fishing guide (fishing reel, get it?). That would explain why he had never had use for a Social Security number, or for filing tax returns. Inventing a life for Arland Reel became, by far, the most interesting part of my day.

But what good was creating a paper life for Arland, if I couldn't say what had happened to him? This is when I began tiptoeing, and then taking giant steps, into what I see now was fraud. My motivation, I want to make clear, was never financial gain. I just wanted to see how far the bureaucracy could be fooled into accepting that Arland Reel was a living man.

In those days before computers, our office first learned of a patient's admission from the green copy of a quadruplicate form called the A9. Most days a courier would deposit a new A9 in our inbox. From there, our office manager would record the name and patient ID number and pass the form to the agent due for a new case. The form contained the information necessary for the R&R Agent to get busy tracking down the patient's funds and income. The A9s were preprinted with the patient id numbers assigned in sequence.

It wasn't like blank A9 forms were kept under lock and key. They were stacked on shelves in the Admissions Office, and whichever clerk was typing up the vitals on a new patient simply took the next form on top of the stack. One morning, I visited the Admissions office, ostensibly to clarify the information on a new patient, and happened to place my patient file on top of the stack. When I left, I took my file along with the top blank A9 form.

I had fun that night typing up the A9 for Arland Reel, filling in the details of his life. He had, it seemed, lived inconspicuously in the little river-front village all his life, taking tourists out on the river to fish most of the year, ice fishing in the bay in the wintertime. He never married, and was excused from military service in World War II because of a hand injury incurred from an outboard propeller. People in the village had recently noted episodes of bizarre behavior involving arguments with customers who weren't there. The county sheriff had been called when he started banging on people's doors in the middle of the night, demanding money he thought he was owed. Two days before, he had arrived at the mental hospital by patrol car for assessment.

Because he was a fisherman, I thought it a nice touch to assign him to River Cottage. The "cottage" was in fact a rambling gray stone building that had originally housed patients assigned to work at the farm on what was called back then the "Lunatic Asylum". Its best feature was a long porch facing the wide river. I thought my Arland Reel would enjoy spending his last days watching the boats go by.

The next morning, I dropped the green copy of the form into the office inbox, and, by being johnny-on-the-spot, assured that the office manager assigned it to me. Then, naturally, I had to get busy working out some financial resources and reimbursement for Mr. Reel.

Since he had no assets, had never served in the military, and never paid into the Social Security System, the only income available for Mr. Reel was Supplemental Security Income, or SSI. I completed the application, naming the psych center's director as representative payee (as she was for all incompetent patients), and sent it off. A month later, I received the notice that he would be awarded $78 a month, of which $13 was reserved as the "Patient Allowance". The rest would be billed for his care. That also made Mr. Reel eligible for Medicaid, so the Office of Mental Hygiene could bill the state Medicaid Office, and I would have all my ducks in a row.

A few days later I received a call from the director's secretary, a woman known for her command of all details related to the hospital's affairs. Agatha was under some embarrassment. Unfortunately, the hospital's copy of Arland Reel's A9 form was missing. Did we have a copy? It was seldom that the therapeutic side of the mental hygiene system called on the reimbursement side for help, so I was only too happy to oblige.

And there matters sat. For the next ten months, I toiled away at my real duties, taking a moment now and then to imagine how my fictional Mr. Reel was faring, and occasionally chuckling to myself that I had been able to create a patient out of whole cloth, or rather, out of quadruplicate forms.

Then one day, shortly before Christmas, I received a call from Carl Mackie, supervisor of the men's ward at River Cottage. He noted that money had built up in Arland Reel's Patient Allowance account, because he never spent any of it. The staff wanted to get a color TV for the ward for Christmas, and would I okay using Mr. Reel's money towards this worthwhile purpose?

I was disappointed by this call. I had always regarded Carl Mackie as a straightforward and honest fellow, and here he was proposing to perform a scam. He obviously knew there was no Arland Reel and thought that made it easy to get hold of his money. Of course, I couldn't say how I knew he was scamming, so I gave my okay. A few weeks later I heard through the grapevine that the ward's patients and staff were enjoying a new color TV.

One day in the spring, when our office manager came back from her daily trip to the mail room, she told me about a package that had arrived there. It was the practice to open all packages that came for patients, and sometimes it was a source of amusement for the mail room staff to see what was inside. That day, the men in the mail room were passing around some bright new fishing lures. The office manager said, "They came in a package for one of your cases, Arland Reel." I was disappointed in Carl Mackie again, figuring that he had just finagled some new fishing gear for himself.

In the fall, I made one of my rare visits to a patient ward, this time to see an old German veteran residing at River cottage. It was an odd and complicated case. The fellow had been a prisoner of war at an upstate POW camp. His paranoid schizophrenia had made it impossible to repatriate him after the war. Now, thirty years on, he seemed to have become rational enough to be returned, and it was my job to work it out. He stood belligerently in the common room, bristling at my questions.

"Believe me, the last place I want to be is here," he told me in a thick accent. "If I could, I would swim right across that river to Canada. My friend Arland says he will take me one day in his boat."

"Your friend Arland?"

"Dah, Arland Reel. You can see him through the window, out there on the porch."

I finished the interview as calmly as I could. Then, feeling considerably rattled, I stepped out on the long porch. The man the German had pointed out was sitting stiffly in a rocking chair, facing the river. He was a very slight man wearing a plaid wool shirt. His face was furrowed in deep lines, and his lowered eyebrows made him look like he was permanently squinting into the sun.

I sat on the porch rail facing him. He didn't seem to notice me. It was as if he was staring right through me to the river. "Mr. Reel," I said, "how are you today?"

No response. He rocked slowly back and forth.

"Is your name really Arland Reel?"

He didn't answer. Then he coughed, and when he brought his right hand up to cover his mouth, I saw that he was missing two fingers.

"Mr. Reel," I said, not liking the nervous tremor in my voice, "How did you happen to come here?"

He was silent for a long time, and just when I thought he wasn't going to reply, he said, "I came from the river, and this is where I am."

I made some more attempts to get him to talk, but a couple of the aides started taking notice of me. I got up to leave before I was asked to go. I said, "I'm going now, Mr. Reel."

He said again, not looking at me, "I came from the river, and this is where I am."

The patient Arland Reel made it through another Christmas and died in the psych center's medical-surgical unit a few days after New Year's. A week later, as was the practice, Carl Mackie and I got together to inventory his belongings. There wasn't much. There were three never-used fishing lures and a couple small black river stones, polished from long handling. His share of the TV was considered to be his gift to the ward.

Months later, on my last day of work at the psych center, I visited Arland Reel's numbered marker in the facility's cemetery. I had to ask a groundskeeper's help to find it. The small square stone held me there for a long time, longer than I had spent at his grave marker where I had first learned his name. Not many people end up with more than one gravestone.

Had I really brought Arland Reel back to life through bureaucratic paperwork? If I did, had I done him a favor?

I hope so.

Candelin Wahl

Born in a Quarter Moon

for Alexandra

Folded like an eggling
past your time,
you slid off the tip
of the quarter moon,

held its curve through
your afternoon debut,
drifted on Mama
skin-to-skin.

Early stars arrived
to twinkle hello—
first hours hushed
as a woodland dawn.

Candelin Wahl

Merry, Merry: A Haibun

Last minute shopping downtown. Snagged a spot that fit my
SUV nose-first. Stepped into slush from yesterday's wet snowstorm. Spied a pair of wire-rimmed frames near the car—no lenses.
Dropped recently, rolled flat by a slow-moving tire. Can't say what
made me lift the ruined spectacles from the cold mess. Dented blue
rims, made in China. Someone's holiday blurred, forced to squint
at cards, recipes, to-do lists. No replacing those specs 'til after
Boxing Day.

Wire-rimmed frames
Crushed, sightless
Holiday a blur

Kerstin Lange

Eastern Sea

The barbed wire between the two German states always went straight through my heart.

– Wolf Biermann, East German singer-songwriter

I sensed the sea in the air before I could see it. The subtle hint of salt, the tangy whiff of seaweed and soggy beach silt. I felt a smile spread over my face. This was what air was supposed to feel like. For a moment, the morning breeze transported me back to the North Sea coast, to the sea of my childhood. To the endless waters and beaches and dunes that gave my childhood a magical sense of freedom.

Strictly speaking, the landscape of my childhood was eighty kilometers inland, at the edge of Bremen, the old port city on the river Weser. Even more strictly speaking, most of my childhood unfolded in an urban setting, centered first on an apartment complex next to an Autobahn, then on a rented townhouse, and finally on the single-family home my parents had dreamed of and saved for all through my first thirteen years. But it was the landscape of the North Sea coast that imprinted itself on my childhood brain the most.

The air that filled my lungs that morning belonged to Germany's other sea, some 150 kilometers farther east: the Baltic Sea, *Ostsee* in German – literally, the Eastern Sea. Steering my bicycle toward the Baltic coast, I could feel anticipation rising about this other, less familiar sea, and about my mission to trace the border that divided this coastline and my home country for forty years.

From 1949 to 1989, most of the Baltic Sea coast lay in East Germany, officially known as the German Democratic Republic, or the GDR – a mysterious country about which I knew almost nothing until it ceased to exist. As a child in the 1960s, I had little reason to wonder why there were two Germanys – it had been that way since before I was born. Occasionally there were news stories about hair-raising escapes from that other Germany – like that of two families who managed to fly over the deadly border strip in a home-made hot air balloon the summer I turned fifteen. And I vaguely knew that my friend Ingeborg's mother had fled from the *Eastern zone*, as West Germans continued to refer to East Germany for years even after both countries declared themselves sovereign states in 1949. The *Ostzone*. Even as a child, I knew that this was not just a geographic reference: the word carried a sad, almost ominous undertone when adults talked about it, a sense of irreversible loss that my child's brain could not grasp.

* * *

On this summer morning, I was glad that the air felt familiar. Glad, too, that this sturdy, black *Bremen Bike* – made in my hometown, as the red manufacturer's decal announced – would be my companion on this border journey. A sensible bike, with mud guards and dynamo hub lights. I liked this bicycle.

It was actually not my own bike but my father's: Having left the country three decades earlier, I had none of my own in Germany. We both knew that he would have been a perfect travel companion on this expedition were it not for his failing eyesight. At seventy-nine, he was still in excellent physical shape, but more and more of his field of vision had vanished from a condition that had plagued him all his life. He had given up car driving years ago, and then the long bicycle trips he loved, too, like the one along the entire Baltic Sea coast he had done with some friends in his early sixties. Now he only rode his bike close to home, on the secret paths he had known for decades. I knew he would miss it. In a way, at least, he might feel like part of him would be with me on this journey.

I had left Bremen earlier in the morning on a train east to Lübeck, whose city limits ran right up against the border with East Germany during the Cold War. Some years ago, when I first started thinking about the border, I had asked a friend from Lübeck what it was like to live so close to it. He said it was eerie and normal at the same time. "It sounds strange now that it's gone," he told me, "but somehow it became part of the landscape."

From Lübeck, it was a short ride on a two-car regional train to Travemünde, a resort town right on the coast and just as close to the former border. I had barely pedaled a half mile from the train station in that exhilarating sea air when my nose picked up another missive: the warm, slightly yeasty aroma of fresh *Brötchen* – breakfast rolls. In all my years living away from Germany, I had never stopped missing this smell. The smell that meant that the world was still *in Ordnung.* Or that even if it wasn't in order, I could at least uphold a modicum of order in my corner of it. Once, many years ago, in my bed in Vermont, I woke up with a sense of that comforting smell and a feeling of deep contentment, and then realized, startled, that it had been part of a dream.

I had not exactly planned to take a break so soon, but if my mission was to reconnect with Germany, a bakery stop was practically mandatory. And this one clearly looked, and smelled, like a winner: the display case nearly burst with at least a dozen different kinds of *Brötchen*, from the plain *Krosse* (crisp one) to the hearty wholegrain *Weltmeister* (world champion) and a number of rolls with maritime names like *Backbord* (portside) and *Anker*. Three cashiers were in constant motion; one of them was wearing a tightly wrapped Muslim headscarf. I knew that headscarf-wearing women were no longer an uncommon sight in Germany in 2017. Neither were comments – often insults – unusual, sometimes voiced directly at the woman, sometimes expressed in online chat forums. That morning in the Travemünde bakery, no one seemed to take special notice.

The tinkly bell that pealed each time a customer entered sounded just like the one at my parents' neighborhood bakery in Bremen. And just like at that bakery, the tinkling was followed by a "Moin," the ubiquitous northern German greeting. Several tables seemed to be filled with regulars; the buzz of conversation mingled with the waft of the fresh *Brötchen*. I didn't know anyone there, but the place pulled me in with a sense of the familiar, of home.

I ordered a *Weltmeister* Brötchen with butter and jam and sat down at a table near the window. Maybe this bakery-café could help me think about home, or even *Heimat*.

Some words have meanings that are easy to translate, but *Heimat* is not one of them. In the Middle Ages, it was a legal term that meant someone had the right to settle and follow their trade in a particular location. The word still has the meaning of home place, or the place a person is from. But most of the meaning of *Heimat* lies below the surface, like the bulk of an iceberg. *Heimat* is inseparably tied to a person's feelings about that geographic place: a sense of belonging, of feeling understood, of connectedness with a particular landscape and familiar people, of not being a stranger, of one's native habitat. People who leave their home place find or create, if they are lucky, a second *Heimat*. Sometimes they feel *heimatlos* (without a home) and miss their *Heimatland* (home country). Always there are gaps between the old *Heimat* and the new: the absence of one's native language on the radio, the separation from loved ones, the elusive smell of fresh *Brötchen*.

And yet, there is a dark side to *Heimat*. Enveloped by the smells and sounds around me, a corner of my mind opened a crack to a different connotation. A meaning that connects *Heimat* with national identity and all too easily spills over into exclusion, even disdain for anyone "other." The Nazis seized on this aspect of *Heimat* and almost managed to poison the term beyond repair. For decades after World War II, young Germans were embarrassed to use the word and avoided it like the plague, except in combined terms like *Heimatstadt* (home city) or *Heimweh* (missing one's home). The rise of the postwar *Heimatfilm* movie genre, with its abundance of dirndls, bright green Bavarian mountain scenes, and kitschy storylines, did little to redeem the word. And now, as I had recently found out from a magazine article, there was a *Heimat* club that artfully mixed anti-foreigner messages into announcements for harvest festivals and bicycle outings, and an initiative that called itself "Zukunft Heimat" (*Heimat* as future) that organized protests against refugee shelters.

* * *

Fortified by my *Brötchen*, I stepped outside, unlocked the bicycle, and set out to find whatever was left of the German-German border's northern end.

The first step was to find the ferry to the Priwall peninsula, which was once cut in half by the border. During the Cold War, the only way to access the Priwall from West Germany was by ferry across the Trave. From the east, where the peninsula is attached to the mainland, only GDR border guards and officials of the *Stasi* – East Germany's secret police – were allowed to set foot on it. For regular East German citizens, the Priwall was off-limits.

Turning a corner, I spotted a sign pointing to the ferry dock at the end of a street lined with red brick buildings. *This is what houses are supposed to look like.* As a child, I used to think that all houses were built of red brick, until I realized that northern Germany's plentiful clay was simply the most logical building material to use.

The ferry ride to the peninsula took less than ten minutes and landed me on Mecklenburg Road, the main road east. Modest bungalows – vacation and weekend homes, by the look of it – arranged in rows and circles sat to the left of the road. The seashore had to be just beyond the gently undulating beach grass covering the dunes.

During the Cold War, Mecklenburg Road had ended at the Iron Curtain. My eyes scanned the sides of the road. I was not exactly sure what I was looking for – an old watchtower? a piece of stretched-metal fence? one of the black-red-yellow border posts with East Germany's hammer-and-compass emblem and the words "Deutsche Demokratische Republik"?

The first clue came from my ears when the even purr of smooth asphalt under my tires gave way to the quietly crunching sound of packed dirt. From the corner of my eye, I spotted a massive boulder to the left of the bike path. I turned around and pushed my bike back to read the inscription:

Never again divided.

A large interpretive sign explained that at this particular location, the border was opened on February 3, 1990. An aerial black-and-white photo next to it showed swarms of people converging on the wintry beach from opposite directions. The photo was grainy, the people in it looked like indistinct ants.

My eyes welled up.

What is this about? Why does this photo from nearly three decades ago move me to tears?

I leaned my bike against the side of the boulder and gazed east, past the almost imperceptible change in Mecklenburg Road's pavement. The vacation homes were behind me now, an unruly miniature forest lined both sides of the road ahead. Wild rose bushes, small willows, poplars, white birches, some stunted white pine; the distinctive warm orange of sea buckthorn berries poked through the countless shades of green. No obvious features in the landscape that would have served as a natural boundary, like a mountain range or a river, though rivers did form part of the "German-German" border farther south. Not that a river or a mountain range ever *had* to be a border.

This particular border was an outcome of World War II, drawn up by the Allied powers to delineate their respective occupation zones. For the first four years after the war, it was merely a demarcation line between the Soviet zone and those of the western Allies. The line only became a border in 1949, when first West Germany, then East Germany declared itself a sovereign state. For a few more years, it was a fairly benign border; people could cross it in both directions with proper identification, for work, family visits, or to buy or sell things. Even people without proper identification or approved purposes would cross, except they would do it in remote places and under cover of darkness.

All of this came to a grinding halt in 1952, when the Soviet-backed East German regime drew up a new set of regulations that, over the years, transformed the border into a strip of land filled with ghastly obstacles, including land mines. From the eastern side, the strip was bordered by a signal fence – named for the wires that would send a silent signal to the guards in the watchtower at the slightest touch. There was a westward fence, too, but that one was set back some fifty meters from the border line itself. *They thought of everything,* I remember thinking when I first saw a model of the installations at a border museum. That fifty-meter strip, called the *outward sovereign territory,* allowed specially authorized border guards to make repairs to the western side of the fence. It also gave them a clear line of sight to follow – and shoot at – escapees.

Gazing into the scraggly little forest along Mecklenburg Road, I thought of the damp-cold March day in 2010 when I first visited the former border some 200 km south of here. I was walking through a stand of Scotch pines when my eyes caught on a simple, weathered wooden cross that blended in with the surrounding forest, its surface reflecting a dark green sheen of lichen growth. I walked closer to read the inscription:

Bernhard Simon

30 Juli 1945 – 28 Oktober 1963

Er wollte von Deutschland nach Deutschland.

He wanted to go from Germany to Germany.

I cannot say how long I stared at the cross, feeling the weight of the border hit me like a fist to the stomach. Bernhard had tried to escape from East Germany with his brother Siegfried that night in October 1963, and stepped on a landmine. The detonation nearly tore off one of his legs. His brother managed to pull him onto West

German soil and tie off his injured leg, but he had to run nearly two miles to get help. Bernhard died on the way to the hospital.

I looked at the aerial photo again, at the tiny dots of people converging on the beach. Yes, it had reminded me of the heavy burden the border had imposed on people's lives. But there was another layer to my tears. Shot through with the grief about the border was the electric joy at its unexpected demise.

* * *

It was late afternoon in upstate New York on November 9, 1989, when a friend practically ordered me to turn on the TV because "something big is going on in Berlin." And so I found myself staring at the screen an ocean away from Germany, speechless, barely comprehending what I was seeing. Throngs of people were crossing through the Berlin Wall, even dancing on top of this forbidding edifice that, only that morning, had been part of the deadliest border regime in the world.

If... if East Germans could simply walk into West Berlin, how would their government be able to keep up the rest of its high-security border system between East and West Germany?

It appeared that the border was history, and what I was watching was that history happening in real time, in the lives of real people.

This seemed surprising. In school, I had gotten the impression that history was the realm of people who had been dead for hundreds of years, if they had ever really been alive at all. The events recounted in textbooks had always seemed inevitable, preordained, as if spooling from an old-fashioned movie reel. Later, I wondered whether the euphoric scenes in Berlin could possibly appear like that in the future. Would future schoolkids hear "On November 9, 1989, the Berlin Wall fell" and not feel the boundless energy of that day? Would they know that the Berlin Wall did not just crumble, but was brought down by a peaceful revolution? That thousands of East German citizens had risked their jobs and their lives to fight for basic civil rights, free elections, and the freedom to travel where they wanted?

Along with the fall of the Berlin Wall, those future schoolkids would also learn that less than a year later – on October 3, 1990 – the two Germanys became one country again. Would they assume that Reunification was the inevitable outcome, that it was the wish of the protesters?

Granted, soon after November 9, 1989, the chants of "We are the people" had turned into "We are one people," but no one could predict what would actually happen. Maybe the two German states would reunite, maybe not. Maybe they would continue to coexist, but now as friendly neighbors with a shared border as unremarkable as those between, say, Vermont and Massachusetts. Or maybe this was a historic chance to try something different altogether.

* * *

On a crisp mid-December day one month later – I had just arrived for the Christmas holidays at my parents' house – some friends and I decided on a whim to see if we could cross into East Germany. We grabbed our passports, thinking we might have a less than a fifty-fifty chance without a visa. In those early days, no one knew what the procedure was at any of the checkpoints: There had been no time yet to come up with a consistent protocol.

As we approached the guard booth and slowed down, passports in hand, my heart raced. What happened next was a complete surprise: the border guard raised his arm and waved us through. We stared at him, we stared at each other – he did not even ask to see the passports! *Was he actually smiling?* It was unbelievable. Crossing into the GDR had taken less than five minutes.

On the *other side*, the road narrowed to a single lane. We deposited the car somewhere in the nearest town, then followed the sounds to where there seemed to be a public event of some kind. As it turned out, the event was an open-air welcome party put on by the people of the town for visiting westerners. Tables laden with baked goods and thermos bottles lined the streets; someone handed us steaming mugs of coffee and plates of home-baked cake; people laughed and cried and said, "Willkommen," over and over again. I had never seen my fellow Germans expressing such unrestrained joy.

The laughing and crying were contagious. Still now, I remember the strange mix of familiarity and culture shock. The people here spoke German, though with an unfamiliar inflection. Thuringian, it must be. Their offerings of coffee and cake felt as German as, well, coffee and cake. But there was something different about the town. The houses were tinged a sad-looking brown and the air smelled like sulphur from the coal-fired furnaces, the cars were smaller and had a goofy toy-car look; the grocery stores were quaint-looking and called *Konsum*.

On a whim we decided to go inside one *Konsum*, where, I am afraid, we gawked like tourists on an exotic vacation. The store was much smaller than those we were used to, the brands were ones we had hardly ever heard of, and there were far fewer choices.

When I said *Auf Wiedersehen* to the storekeeper, I could not quite look her in the eye.

* * *

The fall of the Berlin Wall, the open-air welcome party, the simple memorial for Bernhard Simon: all of these moments returned, triggered by that aerial photograph of the border opening on the beach. *From Germany to Germany.* Sometime after I first read those words on Bernhard's memorial, I had become compelled by this border and resolved to spend some time with it. To find out what the border had meant in the lives of the people who had to live with it, and to learn what traces it had left in the land.

I already knew that most of the military installations had been removed in the early 1990s. But I also knew that the border had left another legacy, and that was what had first compelled me. I had not given much thought to what had become of the former border until the subject came up when I was listening to a German radio station on the internet one day in 2007. Astonished, I learned that over a thousand threatened plant and animal species had thrived in the deadly border strip, and that in December 1989, while most of Germany was caught up in the euphoria over the border's demise, a group of dedicated conservationists from both sides had resolved to turn it into a nature preserve and landscape of remembrance. They called it the *Grünes Band* – the Green Ribbon or Green Belt.

In the time it had taken me to read the interpretive sign and figure out why the grainy photo moved me to tears, about a dozen cars had driven past, crossing from the western federal state of Schleswig-Holstein to the eastern state of Mecklenburg–Western Pomerania. None of the cars stopped or even slowed down. *Do those people know that they just crossed the former Iron Curtain?* Perhaps they were locals who drove across it all the time. Or perhaps they were from other parts of Germany and hadn't noticed the boulder and the inscription. But wouldn't they want to know where the border was? Wouldn't parents want to tell their children that a border had once cut through Germany, and that it had been right here? And that now there was a nature reserve in its place?

* * *

My eyes searched for the line between pavement and packed dirt again. If this was the old border line, the scraggly little forest was once the border strip, and now it was the Green Belt. It did not look spectacular, and it was a far cry from the more mature forests I found so compelling. But how could it, if trees had only been allowed to grow there for barely thirty years?

Besides, what did you expect – Yellowstone Park? Charismatic megafauna? This was going to be a more subtle kind of nature experience. Are less flashy creatures less important? After all, biologists had documented rare plant species like the small pasque flower and marsh gentian right here in the Priwall's section of the Green Belt, along with rare species of birds, butterflies, insects, and amphibians.

Most of them were species I had never seen or heard of. In my urban childhood, I acquired only rough categories like "birds" and "trees" for the natural world. The closest thing to "nature" was a bedraggled-looking tangle of shrubs next to the Autobahn that we kids called the *Wäldchen* – little forest. "The extinction of experience," ecologist Robert Michael Pyle once called that trend in many childhoods – the near absence of contact with nature. I had only begun to connect more closely with the natural world as a young adult, and painstakingly learned as much as I could about the birds, trees, and forests of Vermont. Here, perhaps, was my chance to get to know some of the wild beings in my home country.

Ahead of me, where the road made a sharp right turn inland, a wooden boardwalk led to the left, in the direction of the sea. I locked my bike against a bicycle rack and started walking. On the aerial photo from the day the border opened, the watchtower had stood a short distance to my right. There was no trace of it now.

I continued up the boardwalk through the dunes. As I cleared the small rise, a scene from childhood enveloped me like a piece of home: the white sand, the pale-green beach grass, the deep blue of the sea, the feel of the fresh, slightly salty breeze on my skin.

I took off my sandals and walked faster, down to the water's edge, feeling the old thrill of the wet, firm silt squeezing through between my toes. Scanning the sea, the beach, and the dunes in a 360-degree turn, my eyes could not detect a single trace of the border: not the faintest GDR boundary post, no remains of barricades or warning signs.

Here, several kilometers from the vacation bustle of Travemünde, the beach was nearly empty. With a mild start, I noticed that the few people I saw here were nude. *Not an uncommon sight on a German beach,* I reminded my Americanized sensibilities. And in East Germany, nude bathing had been even more common. A small freedom in the midst of all the restrictions on individual choices.

* * *

I walked east for a bit, then abandoned the wet silt to walk up to the dunes again. Sitting down in a shallow depression to look out at the sea, I tried to visualize what I might have seen from here during the time of the Cold War. Watchtowers for sure, and I knew from my friend Axel, who had grown up near the *Eastern Sea*, that border guards had walked around among the sunbathers, making sure that no one dared to go into the water with a boat or even an air mattress. It would have been too easy to paddle out in hopes of getting picked up by a West German or Danish boat, and that would have constituted the East German crime of *Republikflucht* – escape from the republic.

I thought of Bernhard Simon again. His simple cross was the first memorial I had seen for someone who died along this border, but it would not be the last. I needed a way to honor this essential truth about the Green Belt. Perhaps I was like those Henry David Thoreau described as "Sainte-Terrers," people who

> [...]roved about the country, in the Middle Ages, and asked charity, under pretense of going *a la Sainte Terre,*to the Holy Land, till the children exclaimed, "There goes a Sainte-Terrer," a Saunterer, a Holy-Lander.

While my journey was not aimed at the actual Holy Land, I was quite literally traveling on sacred ground in this landscape of remembrance.

Thoreau had also noted a different meaning behind the word "saunterer," one that I needed to hold in mind, too.

> Some, however, would derive the word from *sans terre*, without land or a home, which, therefore, in the good sense, will mean, having no particular home, but equally at home everywhere. For this is the secret of successful sauntering.

"Sans terre" – "without land or a home." Wasn't this the central question in the lives of those who have left their original home, whether by choice, necessity, or force. Can one ever find another home? Or is it possible to be equally at home everywhere, as Thoreau suggests? What did this mean for *Heimat* at a time when 80 million people roamed around the face of the earth, forcibly displaced from their homes?

I climbed down from my perch in the dune and walked back to the boardwalk to pick up my bike.

As I breathed in the warm scent of pine and salt, the thought pleased me that the little forest around me was the same age as the reunited Germany. Like the biological recovery in the ghastly border, maybe this could be a source of renewal in human lives, too. Whether I spotted any rare critters today or not, from here to the Czech border, this bizarrely shaped 1,400-kilometer-long strip of land – biological corridor and living memorial in one – was here for all of us.

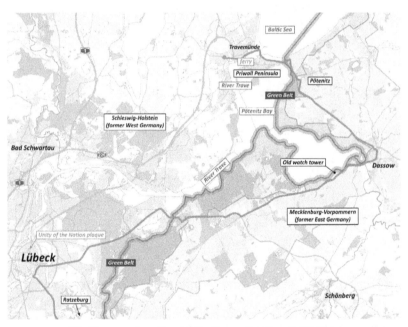

Northernmost section of the former border. Solid line: author's route; Highlighted line: the former border between East and West Germany
Map by Sebastian Steude

Map of Germany showing the former border between East Germany (German Democratic Republic) and West Germany (Federal Republic of Germany)
from "West Germany and the Iron Curtain. Environment, Economy, and Culture in the Borderlands" by Astrid M. Eckert (2019, Oxford University Press)

Mary Schanuel

Hannah Rose

I've loved you, child,
since you were this big
— the space between finger and thumb —
tinier than a grape, shorter than a gasp.

I watched you move and squirm
wriggle tiny fingers and toes.

I saw you with my eyes
and my impatient heart
on that magic silver screen,
a window to your world.

Mary Schanuel

Dusk in the Oak

The robins rush home, landing on the oak
in a great flurry and rustle,
a tittering crowd
a tea party with too few chairs.

They brag in endless chirps.
Latecomers squawk and cajole,
bounce from branch to branch
each demanding her own place.

These feathered souls
know their way, day after day,
find joy in the worm, the nest of twigs
the warm blue egg.

Two oak leaves rattle
in a staccato chatter,

an impossible sound
given the shyness of the breeze.

And now the flock
goes dead-still, hushed
by some secret signal
of the departing light.

Tricia Knoll

Uneven Hems

In praise of the Mother of Muses

Memory wears her gray gown
with an uneven hem to gatherings
where someone may share a story
she learned a different way.
That lack of symmetry endears
her to me. Home, after listening
fatigue, she slips in beside me
to let our dreams
weave fantastical silks
from the sleep
of unremembering.

*

At daybreak she hoists her tools in a cowhide
letter-carrier's bag: socket wrench
and hacksaw, thesaurus, photo album,

field guide, calendar, and mixed-up
twice-told tales, some on cassettes
with no machine to play them. Scissors.
Matches. Called upon, she opens
the faucet so truth can run. Or dribble.

*

She does not claim to be perfect.
Her fingernails rim with dirt
from scratching surfaces. Her knees
bear scars of scrapes and stumbles.
Her running shoes bear mud
from jogging the trail to the bridge
over the train track. I ignore
what flakes off on my rug.

*

She is not my judge. She's my cranny
in the cave for sacred candles.
Her heavy-lidded eyes and tight lips
hint at aching feet and a weary back.
Still – she helps me feel held
in our intimacy of silk.

*

She defends herself from my accusations
that she is a mean editor:

I warned you with slid-away names,
your worm-holed digests. Aging days
tucked away in no-one's-home, but

I bookmarked gold-star hours:
babies bundled. Lake Beautiful.
The wedding where the wedding held.
Sweetie, stories erode.
Bedrock under drip.

I struggle under trickle.

Tricia Knoll

Stealing from the Neighbors

I haul my cart like a horse in traces
to collect rocks from the eight-foot berm

of clay clawed up for their new basement.
After days of rain, my boots clog with mud,

a cart horse bogged in heavy slogging.
I'm picky for the round rocks, striped or gray.

A woman cannot have too many stones.
Garden granite, greenstone.

I'm an old woman loading stones
half-size of bowling balls,

round from long-time tumble. Muttering

geology words I learned in college – dikes,

good veins, pillow lavas, slaty cleavages, bedding, thrust
faults, slip surfaces, naked ledges and lonely erratics.

A sexiness in this muddy venture has me laughing.
The white and buff of dolostone lies treasured in my cart.

If the Earth is our mother, from what I've gathered,
she must have been a fine and goodly hen.

John Sanborn

Home, as it were

I was up all night, with
the uninvited guests
of each little Titanic-infused
drama that scorched my day.

Sleep cast aside by
slights that rankled and grew
and infected, and insults
that kept me awake,
my plotting of revenges,
my regretting words said,
agonizing over words unsaid,
whispered voices of accusations.

Sleep pushed aside,
I walked into all
the dark rooms in my head,
gazing into the lost minutes,

watching the clock and
its pitiless movement.

Of all the places to live,
why did I pick regret?

Sayantani Roy

Tryst

Doc declares the onset
the honeymoon phase as if
disease were a new lover—
the suffering a contract
that shall be upheld and
ploughed through—and in
moments when a leg falls
wayward or fingers can't grasp
steadily you commend to its
uncanny spell that holds
at bay everything else and
thralls body and mind.

So ensnared you're gutted
when another speaks of
their tryst with the same
exacting lover—the one
that has you all wrung out.

Sayantani Roy

On the shores of the Padma

ever done anything illegal/ my friend asks slightly bored/ sure, I deadpan/ have jaywalked/ kept a library book forever/ rode free several times on the jam-packed Sealdah trainline/ you needed a spacesuit to ward off hungry hands/ once put a fresh scratch on a shiny car as I pulled out/ it haunts me still/ and once/ we bribed a tongawalla/ to take us out to the no man's land the border security left unmanned/ my heart kept beat with the horse hooves/ ponies really/ as scrawny as their master/ an old man happy to get a few rupees extra/ we stood at the Padma's shore/ water stretched like a mirage/ distant shore clouded/ my uncle and dad faced the river/ stoic or perhaps unmoved/ and I wished them tears/ for a lost homeland/ for brothers who died there before they were born/ for the Padma's unbreachable breadth.

Andrew Carlo

Conditions are Dire

...that was the report I got from my son upon returning home, after working for a few days in Maine.

He was sitting on his stool at the counter, but I could see what he meant, or at least part of what he meant, from the mudroom. I still had my snowy shoes on and my shoulder bag in my hand, and my computer bag on my shoulder, and my other bag with the dirty clothes and the food containers from the trip and my cell phone in my other hand, and my wallet in my mouth because my hands were full, but I had a pretty good view of the conditions, and I could see how they might have gotten dire while I was in Maine.

He's nineteen years old now and he's not all that chatty to tell the truth, so this was a lot of communication coming right off the bat upon my return from Maine. But despite the conditions, I was thankful for the comment. I love it when we get to talk and for him to initiate a conversation is exceedingly rare, but I don't want to discourage him. Short and simple is how he likes his conversations, so I put down my bags and took the wallet out of my mouth. "How so?" I asked.

For context, I'll mention that it's been quite a few years since the family came running to greet Daddy at the door after being away, and it's been quite a few years since they helped bring stuff in from the truck, or even looked up from their Hulu upon my return, although I'm not complaining. I'm always happy to be back in the warm glow of the family, and happy to do whatever I can to help with the dire conditions, even after my eight-hour drive through the snowstorm, which was blowing a gale.

He doesn't like small talk, or any other kind of talk for that matter, and after a long and painful learning curve I have finally gotten to the point where I can live with that. Actually, I don't like small talk myself so I try to avoid it with him (except for the 'I love you' part, which isn't really small talk anyway, and which I might over-do at times (although I mean it every time). It can make a nineteen-year-old pretty uncomfortable, let me tell you.)

"See for yourself," he said and he pointed with his chin.

There was a substantial pile of dirty dishes in the sink, and more on the counter next to the sink, and more over on the other counter too, and those conditions were indeed dire. This family needs constant reminders like "wash your dishes" and I, being the father and husband, have accepted this as my responsibility (except while working in Maine, because it doesn't go over well by phone, or so I've learned). It's not easy doling out these reminders all the time but I'm just trying to keep conditions from getting dire around here, at least while I am around here.

But I could see it wasn't just the dishes. Conditions were dire here and there all around the kitchen, and just for instance, I'll mention animal hair.

There are two cats and one dog in this household, and the amount of animal hair that builds up in the house over the course of a few days, behind the rocking chair and under the couch, is really astounding. This issue can be quite easily addressed by periodic sweeping and vacuuming, but you can't just sweep in the middle of the room the way some people do. You have to get under the couch and under the desk and behind the rocking chair and around the edges, because that's where the hair is, and it was really built-up there this time. I could see cumulus clouds of animal hair from where I was in the mudroom, behind the rocking chair and along the edge of the wall, just as two examples. I assume it was just as bad or even worse under the couch on which my wife sat. She looked up from her Hulu, blew me a kiss, and returned to her Hulu.

These things, the dishes and the animal hair, are much less of a concern in Maine where I stay in a little house at the place where I'm the forester, or sometimes in the Comfort Inn in Waterville when I have to break up the travel. There are few dogs and no cats for me in Maine, and not much of what you might call a 'dish' to wash. But when I get back here it's mostly the cats for the hair (although the dog is not without fault) and it's mostly certain humans for the dishes. And I might be repeating myself here, or almost repeating myself, but it is just incredible the volume of hair that comes off these animals in a week or so, or even in a few days. But don't take my word for it, just look under the couch.

The dog comes over to sniff me when I return home, and she seems legitimately happy to see me for about ten seconds or so, and then she goes back over to her bed and lies down, a little sour-faced in my opinion. I never bring her presents, like cheese, from Maine, and I think she would love me more if I did. There's a life lesson in that for me because my wife likes cheese too. Goat cheese. I should probably bring her some goat cheese from Maine, when I can.

When I get home the family is about ready for bed, so up they go. And of course the dog needs to go out, so out we go, and we walk around in the snow together for a while, and then we come back in and I sit in the kitchen. The hall light goes off upstairs. The house gets pretty quiet.

It's just me and the dog here in the kitchen. Me on the couch and the dog...well, the dog doesn't lie down on her bed like she's supposed to. She just stands there in the middle of the room and looks at me. We just went out and peed, so that can't be the problem. I suspect that something else is afoot.

I go upstairs to report the progress with the dog (the peeing) and the issue with the dog (the just standing there) to my wife. Maybe she can tell me what to do about it.

She's reading in bed.

"Yes," she says, "While you were gone she got away and went over to the neighbor's and ate something from the farm, and I had to go after her because you weren't here. But she ran up the hill into the woods dragging something that looked like a leg. I had to run after her."

"Did you tell her that she's a bad dog when you got her back?" I ask. It seems like a reasonable question.

I see my wife's gaze rise a few degrees above the book. It levels and then she looks straight ahead. She inhales. "When the dog is running away from you like that you can't discipline her, you can't yell at her, and you can't call her a 'bad dog'. She's not a bad dog, she's just a dog being a dog, and if you yell at her you'll scare her and then she'll run away from you even more. Only a mean old man or an idiot would even think about telling her she's a bad dog at a time like that. She's been pacing the floor all night and now you'll have to deal with it." And with that, she closes the book, rolls over and turns out the light.

"Ah," I say, in the dark. "I see."

You might think that comments like that, the idiot and mean old man comments, would make some people say (or at least think), "I know what you mean about the dog, dear, but about what you said about me, being an idiot and all. I don't think that's really *fair*. To me. Perhaps that's not how you would put it, were it not for chemo. Perhaps that's just the chemotherapy talking."

And that might be a *fair* thing to say, or at least think sometimes.

But right now, *fair* has nothing to do with it. *Fair*, as we have learned through our own life lessons, has nothing to do with anything right now. In fact, *fair* is not something we talk about around here anymore. Instead, we try to talk about what works, and we talk about what makes things better, or at least we try to. And we try not to be idiots. So I ask about the rummage sale.

Yes, the rummage sale at the Congregational Church is back after the pandemic. And yes, it happened on the Saturday while I was away in Maine. And yes, my wife and son went, and yes, it was a triumph for the family. Here is the report from my wife:

"B-" (that's our son) "got a pouch with an incredible number of pockets in it. It's upwards of about ten pockets and he's going to keep his pot and all his pot stuff in it. And I got a pair of pants which I thought were high-waisted, but turned out not to be as high-waisted as I thought, but were pretty high-waisted anyway, so they weren't exactly what I wanted but I'll make them work one way or another. And I got you a nice shirt and I got a menorah that W-" (that's our daughter...she's off with her new partner in Massachusetts now) "wants for the spirituality or something."

"OK," I say. "That sounds good," and I really mean it.

We kiss goodnight.

The rummage sale is a special time of year and now I'm sorry I missed it, but that's just the way it goes sometimes. And sometimes, I think to myself in the dark, it's nice to talk about things like this in the dark, things that make life a little better. Things like a Congregational Church rummage sale. And talking about such things in the dark, at bedtime, ends the day on a high note here in the warm glow of the family.

It's peaceful now. And quiet.

No treatments until Thursday.

And now I hear the dog.

Downstairs. She makes the four noises at regular intervals with her throat. It's a sound I've heard many times before. It's a sound I associate with family, with home, with us. At the end of the fourth noise, she throws up.

My wife rolls back over, towards me. She speaks:

"You deal with that."

Contributors

Authors

Andrew Carlo is a husband, father, and forester who lives in Huntington, Vermont. He writes mostly about his parents but sometimes about other things that seem important. He likes sugaring and cutting firewood. His heroes are his parents (Joyce and Don Carlo), Henry Knox, Frederick Law Olmstead, Leon Russell, and Theodate Pope Riddle.

Brian Gardam resumed writing fiction after a career in health administration, where he says his writing was confined largely to grant proposals and annual reports. He lives with his wife in Northern New York and Southern Florida, where he divides his time between writing, bicycle riding, taking dance classes, community volunteering, and reading. He is currently workshopping a novel with the Long Form Fiction Group of the Burlington Writers Workshop. He reports that "Arland Reel" originated as a campfire tale in the Adirondacks.

N.G. Haiduck has been published in numerous journals, most recently, in *Flying South 2022* and *Shorts* (August 2022). Haiduck's first book, *Cabbie: True Tales about Driving a cab in New York City in*

1972, is forthcoming from Finishing Line Press. Among her awards: Jerome Lowell DeJur award in Creative Writing from The City College of New York, BRIO (Bronx Recognizes Its Own) Award from Bronx Arts Council, and Janice Farrell Prize from the National League of American Pen Women. After living in the Bronx for many years, she and her husband, clarinetist Neal Haiduck, recently moved to Burlington, Vermont.

Dorian Hastings and her family, after three hundred years, left Louisiana and now live in a little half-burnt town in Southern Oregon. She has otherwise lived and traveled widely, including stints in Corfu, Boston, New York City, and Sewanee, Tennessee. Her work has been published in *Exquisite Corpse* and *Silk Road Review*.

Tricia Knoll lives in the woods in Williston, Vermont. Her work appears widely in journals and anthologies. *How I Learned To Be White* received the 2018 Human Relations Indie Book Award for Motivational Poetry. *One Bent Twig* (FutureCycle Press) poems honor trees Knoll has planted and lamented in climate change, released in 2023. *Let's Hear It for the Horses* (The Poetry Box) contains love poems for horses. Two more are in the works (*Wild Apples* from Fernwood Press and *The Unknown Daughter* from Kelsay Books) in 2023. Knoll is a Contributing Editor for Verse Virtual. Website: triciaknoll.com

Kerstin Lange is an independent writer and journalist based in Vermont and Germany. Originally from northern Germany, she earned an M.A. in Anthropology from Binghamton University and an M.S. in Natural History/Ecological Planning from the University of Vermont. Her professional path encompasses teaching, educational tour design and guiding, natural history consulting, and print and radio journalism. Kerstin is currently working on a book about the human and ecological echoes of the Iron Curtain. Kerstin's mission in her writing is to make history and ecology personal.

Sharon Lopez Mooney, poet, is a retired Interfaith Chaplain from the End of Life field, living in Mexico and the USA. In '78 Mooney received a CAC Grant for rural poetry; co-published an anthology; co-owned an alternative literature service. She was a "Best of the Net" nominee, chosen "Editor's Choice", and "Elite Writer's Status" in 2022, and she facilitates a poetry workshop. Mooney's poems are published nationally & internationally in journals such as *Glassworks, The Blotter, Umbrella Factory Magazine, MuddyRiver Review, Revue {R}évolution, Avalon Literary, Ricochet, Ginosko, California Quarterly, Galway Review, Cold Lake Anthology, Roundtable Literary Journal, Existere, Soul-lit, El Portal Journal,* and several anthologies. Mooney's poems at: www.sharonlopezmooney.com

Mike Magluilo is a writer and a recovering finance professional, a father of three, and a husband of one. He enjoys clean living and dirty jokes and loves old dogs and small gestures. Mike is the author of the upcoming novel *A Reason to Run* (Rootstock Publishing), and his work has appeared in *Zig Zag Lit Ma*g and *Cold Lake Anthology.* His short fiction and essays can be found on his website MikeMagluilo.com. He lives in Cornwall, Vermont.

Mark Pendergrast is the author of many nonfiction works, including *For God, Country and Coca-Cola,* Uncommon Grounds, Mirror Mirror, *Inside the Outbreaks, Memory Warp,* and others. He has also written several children's books, including *Jack and the Bean Soup* and *Silly Sadie*. He writes poetry when so inspired from his home in Burlington, Vermont.

Sayantani Roy's writing straddles both India and the US, and she calls both places home. She is an ESL teacher and a reading buddy, and she hopes to teach poetry to young children one day. Her writing has been published in *The Seattle Times*.

John Sanborn is a life-long resident of Vermont. He has had many professions – a teacher of all grades, a retired Army veteran, a CPA for twenty-six years, and lastly, a retired Pastor, hospital and Hospice Chaplain for the last fourteen years. He now enjoys retirement with his wife, Deborah.

Mary Schanuel has been a writer since she could hold a pencil and has published her work since she was eighteen. Her short fiction, poetry, and nonfiction have been published by the *New York Times* "At Home" and "Letters," *Working Mother, Organic Gardening, Los Angeles Daily News, The Heartbeat, Feral: A Journal of Poetry and Art, FictionWeek Literary Review, LifeSherpa,* and *St. Louis Public Radio*. She has written two novels, and her poetry and prose were featured in *In the Moment - Writing from a Spacious Mind*, an anthology of the Missouri Zen Writers.

Candelin Wahl is an emerging Vermont poet, songwriter, and former Poetry Editor for *Mud Season Review*. She thanks the nonprofit Burlington Writers Workshop for years of encouragement and craft-building workshops. Also, instructor extraordinaire Stephen Leslie for sharing the wonders of haiku and haibun writing. To read her published works and blog musings, please visit www.candelinwahl.com.

Cover Art

Susan Smereka was born and raised outside of Toronto, Ontario and has lived in Vermont for over thirty years. Susan graduated from Concordia University, Montreal with a BFA in 1994. Whether working at the etching press with ink and collage, writing and bookmaking, or creating video installations, Susan is interested in the concepts of disorganization and coherence and reconciling these opposites, a process that has engaged her for over 40 years. Smereka co-founded **new new art studio** in 2020 with her partner, Kevin Donegan. **new new art studio,** Burlington, is a space for teaching, exhibitions, and the creation of fine art.

Susan exhibited monoprints and paintings at the AVA Gallery, Lebanon, NH; installations and groups shows at the Flynndog, Burlington, VT; solo show of paintings at Rhombus Gallery, Burlington, VT; and paintings at the Firehouse Gallery, Burlington, VT. Smereka's grants and residencies include Development Grant from the Vermont Arts Council, 2009; Creation Grant from the Vermont Arts Council, Rotary International Group Study program in India, 2004; Kittredge Foundation Grant, 2002; Incentive Grants from the Vermont Arts Council, 2001 and 2002; three month residency in Taos, New Mexico, from the Helene Wurlitzer Foundation, 1998 and 2008; and a three month residency at the Vermont Studio Center, 1996.

Acknowledgements

The Burlington Writers Workshop recognizes the hard work and commitment of the members of our writing community, who work with one another to refine and improve their writing craft. We acknowledge our workshop leaders for encouraging the artistic process, fostering collaboration and feedback in our writing groups, and providing a rich cultural forum for the literary arts. We thank the Burlington Writers Workshop Board of Directors and Leadership Team for their dedication and service to our community of writers.

Most especially, we appreciate the writers who have contributed to this year's anthology and Susan Smereka for the beautiful cover art.